Best Loved Fairy Tales

ILLUSTRATED BY FRANK ADAMS

Bracken Books

LONDON

First Published
by Blackie & Sons Limited, London and Glasgow
as *Some Old Nursery Tales*.

This edition published 1986 by Bracken Books,
a division of Bestseller Publications Limited, Brent House,
24 Friern Park, London N12 9DA, England.

ISBN 1 85170 032 3

Printed by Kultura, Hungary.

Jack · and · the · Beanstalk ·

JACK was the only son of a poor widow woman; he was a lazy and extravagant lad, and did not realize that he should have been working to support his mother instead of leaving her to work for him. At length they had nothing left but a cow, and the poor woman sent Jack to sell it at the neighbouring market.

As he was going along, Jack met a butcher, who, finding he wished to sell the cow, offered in exchange for it a hatful of curious coloured beans. Jack thought this a fine bargain, and hurried home to his mother. The poor, disappointed woman upbraided him angrily, kicked the beans in a passion out of the cottage door, and they both went supperless to bed.

Early next morning Jack woke to find leaves shadowing his window. He ran downstairs, and saw that some of the beans had taken root and sprung up to a great height. The immense stalks had so entwined that they formed a ladder, the top of which seemed to be lost in the clouds.

96

Jack set out climbing, and reached the top of the bean-stalk quite exhausted. Looking around, he found himself in a strange, barren country, not a tree, shrub, house, or living thing to be seen. However, he walked on, hoping to see a house where he might beg something to eat and drink. Presently an infirm-looking woman approached: he saw that she was old and poor. She accosted Jack, enquiring how he came there; and he related the circumstances of the beanstalk. She then asked if he recollected his father. He replied that he did not, and added that there must be some secret relating to him, for he had frequently asked his mother who his father was, whereupon she always burst into tears, and appeared violently agitated. The old woman replied:

"I will reveal the whole story; your mother must not. But, before I begin, I require a solemn promise on your part to do what I command. I am a fairy, and if you do not perform exactly what I require, your mother and yourself shall both be destroyed."

Jack promised to fulfil her injunctions exactly, and the fairy continued:

"Your father, though only a private gentleman, was as rich as a prince, and deserved all he possessed, for he only lived to do good. There lived, a great many miles off, a giant who was altogether as wicked as your father was good; who was in his heart envious, covetous, and cruel, but who had the art of concealing those vices.

"Hearing of your father, he was determined to worm

"An infirm-looking woman approached"

himself into his favour. Your father credited the lying story he told, gave him handsome apartments in his own house, and caused him and his wife to be treated like visitors of consequence.

"One day the giant looked out of the window and saw a fleet of ships in distress off the rocks. He hastened to your father and told him to send off all the servants to the rescue. Your father did so and remained alone in the study with the giant. Then the cruel giant stabbed your father in the back, and your father instantly fell dead.

"Your poor mother, when she discovered this horrible

crime, managed to escape from the house with you, a baby three months old, in her arms. She settled in the cottage where you were brought up; and it was owing to her fear of the giant that she has never mentioned your father to you

"I became your father's guardian at his birth; but fairies have laws to which they are subject as well as mortals. A short time before the giant went to your father's, I transgressed; my punishment was a total suspension of power for a limited time—an unfortunate circumstance, as it prevented my helping your father. The day on which you met the butcher, as you went to sell your mother's cow, my power was restored. It was I who secretly prompted you to take the beans in exchange for the cow. By my power the beanstalk grew to so great a height and formed a ladder.

"The giant lives in this country. You are the person appointed to punish him for all his wickedness. You will have dangers and difficulties to encounter, but must persevere in avenging the death of your father, or you will always be miserable. As to the giant's possessions, you may seize all with impunity, for everything he has is yours. Go along the road; you will soon see the house where your cruel enemy lives. Remember the severe punishment that awaits you if you disobey my commands."

So saying, the fairy disappeared, leaving Jack to pursue his journey.

He walked until after sunset, and soon, to his great joy, spied a large mansion. A plain-looking woman was standing at the door. He accosted her, begging she would give him a morsel of bread and a night's lodging. She expressed great surprise on seeing him, said it was quite uncommon to see a human being near their house, for it was well known that her husband was a large and powerful giant, and that he would never eat anything but human flesh if he could possibly get it; that he did not think anything of walking fifty miles to procure it, usually being out all day for that purpose.

Jack hoped to elude the giant, and again entreated the woman to take him in for one night only, and hide him in the oven. The woman at last suffered herself to be persuaded. She gave him plenty to eat and drink, and took him into the house.

A long gallery through which they passed was very dark, just light enough to show that, instead of a wall on one side, there was a grating of iron which parted off a dismal dungeon, whence issued the groans of poor victims whom the giant reserved in confinement for his own voracious appetite. Poor Jack was half-dead with fear, and gave himself up for lost. At the farther end of the gallery there was a winding staircase, which led them into a spacious kitchen. A good fire was burning in the grate, and Jack, not seeing anything to make him uncomfortable here, forgot his fears, and was beginning to enjoy himself, when he was aroused by a loud knocking at the house door. The giant's wife ran to secure him in the oven, and then made what haste she could to let her husband in, and Jack heard him accost her in a voice like thunder, saying:

" Poor Jack was half-dead with fear "

"Wife, I smell fresh meat!"

"Oh, my dear," she replied, "it is nothing but the people in the dungeon!"

The giant appeared to believe her, and walked down-stairs into the very kitchen where poor Jack was, who shook, trembled, and was more terrified than he had yet been. At last the monster seated himself by the fireside, whilst his wife prepared supper. By degrees Jack recovered himself sufficiently to look at the giant through a crevice. When supper was ended, the giant desired his wife to bring him his hen. A beautiful hen was brought, and placed upon the table. Jack observed that every time the giant said "Lay!" the hen laid an egg of solid gold. The giant amused him-self a long time with the hen; meanwhile his wife went to bed. At length the giant fell fast asleep by the fireside, and snored heavily.

At daybreak, Jack, finding the giant not likely to be soon roused, crept softly out of his hiding-place, seized the hen, and ran off with her. He easily found the way to the beanstalk, and climbed down quickly. His mother was overjoyed to see him.

"And now, Mother," said he, "I have brought home that which will quickly make you rich without any trouble. I hope I have made you some amends for the affliction I have caused you through my idleness, extravagance, and folly."

The hen produced them as many eggs as they desired; they sold them, and in a little time became very rich.

For some months Jack and his mother lived happily

together; but he longed to climb the beanstalk, and pay the giant another visit, in order to carry off some more of his treasures. A few mornings later he rose very early, put on a disguise, and, unperceived by anyone, climbed the beanstalk. He was greatly fatigued when he reached the top, and very hungry. He reached the giant's castle late in the evening; the woman was standing at the door as usual. Jack accosted her, at the same time telling her a pitiful tale, and requested that she would give him victuals and drink, and a night's lodging. She told him, what he knew before, concerning her husband, and also that she one night admitted a poor, hungry, distressed boy, who was half-dead with travelling; that he stole one of the giant's treasures; and that her husband ever since was worse than before, and used her very cruelly, upbraiding her continually with being the cause of his loss. Jack did his best to persuade the woman to admit him, and found it a very hard task; but at last she consented, and, as she led the way, Jack observed that everything was just as before. She took him into the kitchen, and hid him in an old lumber closet. The giant returned at the usual time, and walked in so heavily that the house was shaken to the foundation. He seated himself by the fire, saying:

"I smell fresh meat!"

The wife replied that it was the crows, who had brought a piece of carrion, and laid it at the top of the house upon the leads.

While supper was preparing, the giant was very ill-

"The giant reckoned all the money over and over again"

tempered and impatient, frequently lifting up his hand to strike his wife for not being quick enough. She, however, was always so fortunate as to elude the blow. He was also continually upbraiding her with the loss of his hen. Then, having eaten till he was quite satisfied, he said to his wife:

"I must have something to amuse me, either my bags of money or my harp."

After a great deal of ill humour, and having teased his wife some time, he commanded her to bring his bags of gold and silver. Jack, as before, peeped out, and presently the woman brought two bags into the room; they were of an immense size—one filled with new guineas, the other with new shillings. They were placed before the giant. Then the wife went to bed, leaving him to count over his treasures by way of amusement.

First the silver then the gold was taken out of the bags and heaped up on the table. The giant reckoned all the money over and over again, and Jack heartily wished this wealth in his own possession.

Soon the giant fell into a deep sleep, and Jack, creeping out from his hiding-place, seized the bags of silver and gold, and crept quietly out of the house.

Jack was overjoyed when he found himself near the beanstalk; he soon reached the bottom, and immediately ran to seek his mother. An old woman said she was at a neighbour's, ill of a fever, and directed him to the house where she lay. He was shocked on finding her apparently dying, and could scarcely bear his own reflections on knowing himself to be the cause. On being told of his return, she began to recover gradually. Jack presented her with his two bags, and they lived happily and comfortably for some time.

But Jack could not get the beanstalk out of his mind. He brooded over it in secret, and found it hard to satisfy his mother when she asked him the reason for his unhappiness. At last one morning he climbed up the beanstalk again. He found the road and journey much as before. He arrived at the giant's mansion late in the evening, and saw the wife standing at the door. Jack had disguised himself so completely that she did not appear to have the least recollection of him. However, when he pleaded hunger and poverty in order to gain admittance, he found it very difficult indeed to persuade her. At last he prevailed, and was concealed in the copper. When the giant returned in the evening, he said:

"I smell fresh meat!"

Jack felt quite composed, as he had said so before and was soon satisfied: however, the giant seemed to suspect something. For he started up suddenly and searched all round the room until he got to the copper. Poor Jack thought his last hour had come, and only breathed freely when the giant, without removing the lid of the copper, went and sat again at the table.

The giant at last ate a great supper. When he had finished his meal he commanded his wife to fetch his harp. Jack peeped under the copper lid, and saw the most wonderful and beautiful harp that could be imagined. The giant said "Play!" and it instantly played without being touched. The music was very fine; Jack was delighted, for he had never heard anything like it before, and felt more anxious to get the magic harp into his possession than either of the former treasures. The sweet music lulled the giant into a sound sleep, and the woman went into the back-kitchen. Jack quickly made up his mind, got out of the copper, and took the harp. The harp, however, was a fairy, and called out loudly: "Master! master! master!"

The giant awoke, and reeling with sleep, started off in pursuit of Jack. The boy ran as fast as he could, and was lucky to reach the beanstalk first.

" The heavy fall killed him "

The moment Jack set his foot on the beanstalk he called at the top of his voice for a hatchet. One was brought directly. He soon reached the ground. Just at that instant the giant was beginning to come down; but Jack, with his hatchet, cut the beanstalk close off to the root, which made the giant fall headlong into the garden, and the heavy fall killed him.

Jack's mother was delighted when she saw the beanstalk destroyed and the wicked giant overcome. At that instant the good fairy appeared; she first addressed Jack's mother, and explained every circumstance relating to the journeys up the great beanstalk. The fairy then charged Jack to be a dutiful and affectionate son to his mother, and to follow his father's good example in everything, which was the only way to be respectable and happy in this life. After giving this advice she took her leave of them and disappeared from their sight. Jack humbly and with his whole heart begged his mother's pardon for all the sorrow and affliction he had caused her, promising faithfully to be very dutiful and obedient to her for the future. He proved as good as his word, and was a pattern of affectionate behaviour and attention to parents. His mother and he lived together a great many years, and continued to be always very happy.

The Three·Little·Pigs

ONCE upon a time there were three little pigs whose mother was too poor to give them all as much food as they wanted. So, when they were big enough to take care of themselves, she turned them out of the home-sty to find their own living.

As the first little pig trudged through the world, seeking his fortune, he met a man carrying a truss of straw. "If you please, sir," said he, "will you give me that straw to build a house with?"

And, because of his good manners, the man gave him the truss of straw, and the little pig built a house with it, and sat down inside.

By and by a wolf came along, and, smelling the pig, said: "Little Pig, Little Pig, let me come in."

So he huffed, and he puffed, till he blew the house in

But the pig knew the wolf's voice, so he replied: "No, no, by the hair on my chinny-chin-chin!"

"Then," said the wolf, "I'll huff, and I'll puff, and I'll blow your house in." So he huffed, and he puffed, till he blew the house of straw in; and then he ate up the little pig.

As the second little pig trudged through the world, seeking his fortune, he met a man carrying a bundle of furze.

"If you please, sir," said he, "will you give me that bundle of furze to build a house with?"

And, because he was polite, the man gave him the bundle of furze, and the little pig built a house, and sat down inside it.

THE THREE LITTLE PIGS

By and by the wolf came along, and saw the house, and smelt the pig. Then he knocked at the door, and said: "Little Pig, Little Pig, let me come in."

But the pig peeped through the keyhole and saw the wolf's ears, so he replied: "No, no, by the hair on my chinny-chin-chin!"

"Then," said the wolf, "I'll huff, and I'll puff, and I'll blow your house in." So he huffed and he puffed, and he huffed and he puffed, till at last he blew the house of furze in; and then he ate up the little pig.

As the third little pig trudged through the world, seeking his fortune, he met a man carrying a load of bricks.

"If you please, sir," said he, "will you give me those bricks to build a house with?"

And, because he was well-behaved, the man gave him the load of bricks, and the little pig built a house, and sat down inside it.

By and by the wolf came along, and saw the house, and smelt the pig. Then he knocked at the door, and said:

"Little Pig, Little Pig, let me come in."

But the pig peeped through the crack under the door, and saw the wolf's paws, so he replied, as his brothers had done: "No, no, by the hair on my chinny-chin-chin!"

"Then," said the wolf, "I'll huff, and I'll puff, and I'll blow your house in." So he huffed and he puffed, and he huffed and he puffed, and he huffed and he puffed, till he was out of breath; but he could not blow the house of bricks in. And, when he saw that after all his huffing and puffing the house stood firm, he said: "Little Pig, Little Pig, I can tell you where there are some nice turnips."

"Where?" asked the little pig, still safe inside.

"In the field at the top of the lane," replied the cunning wolf, "and, if you will be ready at six o'clock to-morrow morning, we will get some for dinner."

"Yes, I will be ready," said the little pig.

Next day, the little pig got up at five o'clock, and ran quickly to the field at the top of the lane and found some turnips, which he took home for dinner.

At six o'clock the wolf knocked at the door, and said: "Little Pig, I am waiting for you."

"Pray don't wait any longer," replied the little pig, "for I have been to the field and come back, and I have a big dish of nice turnips for dinner."

When the wolf heard this he felt very angry, but he made his voice smooth, and said: "Little Pig, Little Pig, I know where there are some nice apples."

"Where?" asked the little pig, without opening the door.

"On a tree at the bottom of the lane," replied the wolf, "and, if you will be ready at five o'clock to-morrow morning, I will take you there, and we will get some for dinner."

"Yes, I will be ready," said the little pig.

Next day the little pig got up at four o'clock, and hurried to the bottom of the lane and climbed the apple-tree. He had picked a lot of nice apples, and was just going to jump down and run home, when he saw the wolf coming. So he stayed where he was, feeling very frightened. The wolf came to the foot of the tree, and grinned till he showed all his sharp teeth.

"Little Pig," said he, "why did you not wait for me?"

"I was so hungry that I could not wait," replied the little pig. "Let me throw you down one of the apples, that you may taste it, and see how nice they are." And he threw an apple so far that, while the wolf was gone to pick it up, he had time to jump down from the tree and run away home.

"Little Pig, why did you not wait for me?"

Next day the wolf came again to the pig's house, and knocked at the door, and said: "Little Pig, Little Pig, there is to be a fair on the hill this afternoon. Will you go with me?"

"Yes," replied the little pig, "I will go. What time will you call for me?"

"At three o'clock," replied the wolf.

But, as usual, the little pig started before the wolf came, and visited the fair, where he bought a butter-churn. He was carrying it home, when he saw the wolf a long way off, trotting up the hill. Then, as he was very frightened, and could think of nothing better to do, he hid himself in the churn. But, as he jumped in, the churn fell on its side, and began to roll over and over down the hill, with the pig inside.

The wolf, seeing a strange round thing coming towards him, was so much alarmed that he ran away home as fast as his legs would take him, without visiting the fair.

At the bottom of the hill the little pig got out of the churn, and went into his house; and, soon after he was safely inside, the wolf knocked at the door, and said: "Little Pig, I could not go to the fair, for a great round thing ran after me down the hill, and drove me home."

"Ha!" replied the little pig, with a chuckle, "that was my butter-churn, which I bought at the fair; and I was inside it."

Then the wolf was very angry, and declared that he would climb down the chimney of the house, and eat the little pig up; and he began to scramble on to the roof. But, while he did this, the little pig stirred the fire to a blaze, and hung a large pot full of water over it. And, when he heard a noise in the chimney, he lifted the lid of the pot, and the wolf tumbled into the water with a splash. Then the little pig boiled him, and ate him for supper. And after that he lived happily for the rest of his life in the house of bricks.

JACK the Giant-Killer

IN olden times there lived in Cornwall many wicked giants, who were the terror of the country, being so fierce and cruel that no man dared to face them.

But there was a bold boy named Jack, who determined to fight and slay the giants, especially the great giant Cormoran, who lived in a huge castle by the sea. So one night he took a horn, a pickaxe, and a shovel; and, digging a pit outside the giant's castle, he covered it with straw and with the boughs of trees. Then he blew his horn, and the giant, rushing out, fell into the pit and was killed. Jack went down into the pit and cut off the giant's head; and the people called him "Jack the Giant-Killer", and gave him a belt on which was engraved:

"This is the valiant Cornishman
Who killed the giant Cormoran",

58

The giant brought his club and banged at the bed

Now, Cormoran's brother, finding Jack asleep one day in a wood, seized him and threw him into his castle, and called another giant to a feast. But as the giants were passing under Jack's window, he flung out a rope, with a strong noose at each end of it, and, catching them by the head, he strangled them.

And when King Arthur heard of this deed, he made Jack a Knight of the Round Table, and our hero rode through the land with noble knights, killing many giants.

Once he came to a great house, kept by a giant with two heads. This giant was extremely polite, and after supper gave Jack his own bed to sleep in. But Jack, fearing mischief, crept out of the bed; and it was well that he did so, for in the middle of the night the giant brought his club and banged at the bed, hoping that he had put an end to Jack. And, when he saw the youth next morning, he was greatly surprised and disappointed.

"How did you sleep?" he asked.

"Pretty well," said Jack, "except for the rats."

The giant then filled two bowls with porridge, one for himself and one for Jack; but Jack managed to ladle his share into a leather bag inside his waistcoat, and presently said: "See what I can do!" cutting the bag with his sword, so that the porridge fell out upon the floor.

"I can do that too!" roared the giant, and, plunging a knife into himself, he fell down dead.

Now, Jack had an invisible coat and shoes of swiftness, which he had taken from a giant. One day he came to

the castle of a hideous giant with a huge head. A beautiful lady, a knight, and a duke's daughter were prisoners in the castle; but, while the giant was away from home, Jack freed them with one stroke of his sword, and took them back to the knight's castle, where a great feast was given in his honour.

In the middle of the feast, a herald announced that a terrible giant, named Thundel, was approaching.

Now, the castle was surrounded by a moat, across which there ran a drawbridge, so Jack set men to saw through the bridge at one end. Then, putting on the invisible coat and the shoes of swiftness, he went boldly to meet the giant.

At first he led Thundel a dance all round the castle; then, suddenly throwing off the invisible coat, he ran over the bridge with great swiftness, and reached the castle safely. When the giant tried to follow, the bridge fell beneath his great weight, and he was drowned. And the land was not plagued with giants any more.

Jack took the duke's daughter back to her own home, and her father gave her to him in marriage, as a fitting reward for his great courage.

He gave him also a beautiful castle in Cornwall, and there Jack and his bride lived happily ever after.

The·Three·Bears

ONCE upon a time three bears lived in a cottage near a wood.

And in a house on the other side of the wood a little girl lived with her parents.

One of the bears was a GREAT BIG BEAR.

One was a MIDDLE-SIZED BEAR.

And one was a TINY WEE BEAR.

The little girl had long golden hair, so she was called Goldilocks.

One day the three bears went for a walk in the wood, while their breakfast porridge was cooling; and while they were gone, Goldilocks, who was also in the wood, came to their cottage. Noticing that the door was open, she peeped in; and there she saw a table upon which were three bowls of porridge.

One of the bowls was a great big bowl.

60 b

THE THREE BEARS

One was a middle-sized bowl.

And one was a tiny wee bowl.

Set round the table were three chairs.

One of the chairs was a great big chair.

One was a middle-sized chair.

And one was a tiny wee chair.

Goldilocks looked this way and that way, but she saw no one. So she went into the cottage. And, being hungry, she took up a great big spoon, and helped herself to some porridge from the great big bowl. But she quickly dropped the spoon back into the bowl, for the porridge was too hot, and had burned her tongue.

Then she took up a middle-sized spoon, and helped herself to some porridge from the middle-sized bowl.

But she quickly dropped the spoon back into that bowl also, for the porridge was too cold, and she did not like it.

And last, she took up a tiny wee spoon, and helped herself to some porridge from the tiny wee bowl. Now, the porridge in the tiny wee bowl was just right, neither too hot nor too cold. So very soon Goldilocks had eaten it all up.

Then, being tired, she sat down in the great big chair. But she quickly jumped up again, for the great big cushion in it was too hard.

After that she sat down in the middle-sized chair. But again she quickly jumped up, for the middle-sized cushion in it was too soft.

And last, she sat down in the tiny wee chair. And the tiny wee cushion in the tiny wee chair was just right, neither too hard nor too soft. So Goldilocks went on sitting upon it till the bottom of the chair fell out, and the cushion with it, and she found herself sitting upon the floor.

Then she looked this way and that way, and in one corner of the cottage she noticed some steep stairs.

"I will go up those stairs," said she.

So she went up the steep stairs, and then into a little bedroom.

And there she saw three beds.

She found herself sitting upon the floor

One of the beds was a great big bed.

One was a middle-sized bed.

And one was a tiny wee bed.

Being sleepy, Goldilocks lay down upon the great big bed. But she quickly got up again, for the head of the great big bed was too high.

Then she lay down upon the middle-sized bed; but again she quickly got up, for the foot of the middle-sized bed was too low.

60 c

THE THREE BEARS

And last, she lay down upon the tiny wee bed. Now, the tiny wee bed was just right, neither too high at the head nor too low at the foot. So very soon Goldilocks was fast asleep upon it.

When she had fallen asleep, the three bears came home from their walk in the wood.

First, the Great Big Bear espied his great big spoon standing in the porridge in his great big bowl.

"SOMEONE HAS BEEN TASTING MY PORRIDGE," roared he.

Then the Middle-sized Bear espied her middle-sized spoon standing in the porridge in her middle-sized bowl.

"SOMEONE HAS BEEN TASTING MY PORRIDGE," growled she.

And last, the Tiny Wee Bear espied his tiny wee spoon standing in his empty, tiny wee bowl.

"SOMEONE HAS BEEN TASTING MY PORRIDGE," squeaked he, "AND HAS EATEN IT ALL UP."

By this time the Great Big Bear had noticed that the great big cushion that lay in his great big chair was rumpled.

"SOMEONE HAS BEEN SITTING IN MY CHAIR," roared he.

Then the Middle-sized Bear noticed that the middle-sized cushion that lay in her middle-sized chair was rumpled.

"SOMEONE HAS BEEN SITTING IN MY CHAIR," growled she.

And last, the Tiny Wee Bear noticed that the tiny wee cushion of his tiny wee chair lay upon the floor.

"SOMEONE HAS BEEN SITTING IN MY CHAIR," squeaked he, "AND HAS SAT THE BOTTOM OUT."

The three bears looked this way and that way, but saw no one.

So they went up the steep stairs in the corner, and then into the bedrooom.

And there the Great Big Bear immediately noticed that the bedclothes which covered his great big bed were crumpled.

"SOMEONE HAS BEEN LYING ON MY BED," roared he.

Then the Middle-sized Bear saw that the bedclothes on her middle-sized bed were crumpled.

"SOMEONE HAS BEEN LYING ON MY BED," growled she.

And last, the Tiny Wee Bear saw that the bedclothes on his tiny wee bed were lying in an odd, crumpled heap.

"SOMEONE HAS BEEN LYING ON MY BED," squeaked he, "AND HERE SHE IS!"

Goldilocks was very much frightened to see the three bears.

For a minute she stared at them, while they stared back at her.

Then, jumping from the tiny wee bed, the little girl darted down the stairs, with her golden hair flying around her head.

"Someone has been tasting my porridge," roared he

THE THREE BEARS

And the three bears were so dazzled by the brightness of her hair that they stumbled as they ran after her down the stairs.

When they reached the kitchen, Goldilocks had run out of the cottage door; and, when they reached the door, she was a long way off. And though they ran and ran they did not catch her, for she had run right through the wood, and was safe at home with her parents.

So the three bears went back to their cottage.

The Babes·in·the·Wood

FRANK·ADAMS

THERE once lived in Norfolk a gentleman who was very rich indeed, and who was also very good and kind. He had a wife whom he loved dearly; and they had two little children, a boy and a girl.

You can imagine how happy they were. But, alas! one day the good gentleman and his wife fell ill; and no one could make them better again. When they knew that they were about to die, they thought, not of themselves, but of their two little children.

"What is to become of them?" said the dying man. "Who will take care of them when we are gone?"

Then he thought of his brother, the children's uncle, and sent for him.

"Be good to them, dear brother," said he; "for you are the only friend they have now. Take care of our dear little son and daughter."

THE BABES IN THE WOOD

And the uncle promised that he would be good to them. When their parents were dead, he took the little boy and girl away to live with him; and for a while he seemed to love them, and to do all he could to make them happy. But he was really not a good man at all, and was always thinking of the riches that had been left to the children by their father; for he could not forget that those riches would be his if anything happened to the little boy and girl. And at last, when the poor children had not yet been with him a year and a day, he hired two men who were as wicked as himself to take them away to a dark wood and there kill them.

The pretty babes went gladly enough when the men offered to take them for a ride; and so sweetly did they talk to them that the robbers began to feel sorry they had promised to kill any beings so young and gentle. Indeed, one man declared that he would not kill the children after all. But the other man was determined to do this cruel deed, that he might get the large sum of money which the uncle had promised him. So the two quarrelled, and at last came to blows.

Think how frightened the two pretty children were when they saw the fight! They knew only love and gentleness, and did not understand what all this meant. They were still more afraid when one of the robbers lay dead on the ground—not knowing that he had wished to kill them; and what with hunger and fear they began to weep.

THE BABES IN THE WOOD

The other robber tried to comfort them, and at last he mounted his horse and said: "I will go and get bread for you, so do not cry. Wait here till I come back." And he rode away. But, although he spared their lives, he did not mean to return.

"He will come back soon," said the little ones to each other; and they linked hands and wandered up and down, waiting for him. They watched too, till their eyes were tired, and listened to hear his horse's feet; but he did not return.

At last, when they had wandered about till they were

The two quarrelled, and came to blows

tired, the tiny children lay down in each other's arms, and died.

And the birds and beasts came from their homes in the wood to look at them.

"Their hair is made of the sun," said the little rabbits. "And how soundly they sleep!"

But Robin Redbreast, who loves little children, looked longest of all. "Let us cover them over with our prettiest leaves," said he, "so that nothing may come near to hurt them. We must never play our loudest games here, lest they should awake."

So he called to his friends and companions, and they came flying, one by one.

And each bird brought a leaf, which it laid upon the babes in the wood with gentle, loving touch; and back and forward they flew, till the children were quite covered with beautiful leaves. That was the only grave those children had.

This is the end of the story, little ones, but you must know that the robber who had left the children to die in the wood lost his own life soon after, having committed another cruel crime; and before he died he confessed this story.

As for the wicked uncle, he died in prison, and in great poverty; and I do not think we need be surprised, for people who have wicked thoughts and do wicked deeds do not live happily, nor do they die gently.

Little Red Riding-Hood

ONCE upon a time there lived a country girl, who was the sweetest little creature ever seen. Her grandmother had made for her a pretty red hood, which so became the child that everyone called her Little Red Riding-Hood. One day her mother, having made some cakes, said to her:

"Go, my child, and see how your grandmother does, for I hear she is ill; carry her some of these cakes, and a little pot of butter."

Little Red Riding-Hood, with a basket filled with the cakes and the pot of butter, immediately set out for her grandmother's house, in a village a little distance away.

As she was crossing a wood she met a wolf, who had a mind to eat her up, but dared not do so because of some woodcutters at work near them in the forest. He ventured, however, to ask her whither she was going.

The little girl, not knowing how dangerous it was to talk to a wolf, replied:

"I am going to see my grandmother, and carry her these cakes and a pot of butter."

"Does she live far off?" said the wolf.

"Oh yes!" answered Little Red Riding-Hood; "beyond the mill you see yonder, at the first house in the village."

"Well," said the wolf, "I will go and see her too; I will take this way and you take that, and see which will be there the soonest."

The wolf set out, running as fast as he could, and taking

the nearest way, while the little girl took the longest, and amused herself as she went along with gathering nuts, running after butterflies, and making nosegays of such flowers as she found within her reach.

The wolf soon arrived at the grandmother's cottage, and knocked at the door.

"Who is there?" asked a voice.

"It is your grandchild, Little Red Riding-Hood," said the wolf, counterfeiting her voice; "I have brought you some cakes and a little pot of butter, which Mother has sent you."

The good old woman, who was ill in bed, called out:

"Pull the bobbin, and the latch will go up."

The wolf pulled the bobbin, and the door opened. He sprang upon the poor old grandmother and ate her up.

The wolf then shut the door and laid himself down in the bed, and waited for Little Red Riding-Hood, who arrived soon after. Tap! Tap!

"Who is there?"

She was at first a little frightened at the hoarse voice of the wolf, but, supposing that her grandmother had got a cold, answered:

"It is your grandchild, Little Red Riding-Hood. Mother has sent you some cakes and a little pot of butter."

The wolf called out, softening his voice:

"Pull the bobbin, and the latch will go up."

Little Red Riding-Hood pulled the bobbin, and the door opened.

When she came into the room, the wolf, hiding himself

" I am going to see my grandmother "

under the bedclothes, said, speaking in a feeble voice:

"Put the basket, my child, on the stool; take off your cloak, and come into bed with me."

Little Red Riding-Hood took off her red cloak and stepped into bed, where, wondering to see how her grandmother looked in her nightclothes, she said:

"Grandmother, what great arms you have got!"

"The better to hug thee, my child."

"Grandmother, what great ears you have got!"

"The better to hear thee, my child."

"Grandmother, what great eyes you have got!"

"The better to see thee, my child."

"Grandmother, what great teeth you have got!"

"The better to eat thee up."

But at that moment a woodcutter, who was Red Riding-Hood's father, and had come to take her home, peeped in at the window and saw the wolf about to eat up his child.

He quickly ran in, and soon chopped off the wicked wolf's head with his axe. Then he lifted poor Red Riding-Hood in his arms, and, holding her very tightly, to make her feel quite safe, carried her home.

And as he went along, he sang to her these wise words:

"A little maid
Must be afraid
To do other than her mother told her;
Of idling must be wary,
Of gossiping be chary,
She'll learn prudence by the time that she is older."

Little Chicken Kluk

THERE was once a little chicken called Kluk. A nut fell on his back, and gave him such a blow that he rolled on the ground. So he ran to the hen, and said: "Henny Penny, run; I think all the world is falling!"

"Who has told thee that, little chicken Kluk?"

"Oh, a nut fell on my back, and struck me so that I rolled on the ground!"

"Then let us run," said the hen.

So they ran to the cock, and said: "Cocky Locky, run; I think all the world is falling!"

"Who has told thee that, Henny Penny?"

"Little chicken Kluk."

"Who has told thee that, little chicken Kluk?"

"Oh, a nut fell on my back, and struck me so that I rolled on the ground!"

"Then let us run," said the cock.

So they ran to the duck, and said: "Ducky Lucky, run; I think all the world is falling!"

"Who has told thee that, Cocky Locky?"

"Henny Penny."

"Who has told thee that, Henny Penny?"

"Little chicken Kluk."

"Who has told thee that, little chicken Kluk?"

"Oh, a nut fell on my back, and struck me so that I rolled on the ground!"

"Then let us run," said the duck.

So they ran to the goose, and said: "Goosy Poosy, run; I think all the world is falling!"

"Who has told thee that, Ducky Lucky?"

"Cocky Locky."

"Who has told thee that, Cocky Locky?"

"Henny Penny."

"Who has told thee that, Henny Penny?"

"Little chicken Kluk."

"Who has told thee that, little chicken Kluk?"

"Oh, a nut fell on my back, and struck me so that I rolled on the ground!"

"Then let us run," said the goose.

Then they ran to the fox, and said: "Foxy Coxy, run; I think all the world is falling!"

"Who has told thee that, Goosy Poosy?"

"Ducky Lucky."

"Who has told thee that, Ducky Lucky?"

"Cocky Locky."

"Who has told thee that, Cocky Locky?"

"Henny Penny."

"Who has told thee that, Henny Penny?"

"Little chicken Kluk."

"Who has told thee that, little chicken Kluk?"

"Oh, a nut fell on my back, and struck me so that I rolled on the ground!"

"Then let us run," said the fox.

So they all ran into the wood. Then the fox said: "I must now count and see if I have got you all here. I, Foxy Coxy, one; Goosy Poosy, two; Ducky Lucky, three; Cocky Locky, four; Henny Penny, five; and little chicken Kluk, six; Hei! that one I'll snap up." He then said: "Let us run."

So they ran farther into the wood. Then said he: "Now I must count and see if I have got you all here. I, Foxy Coxy, one; Goosy Poosy, two; Ducky Lucky, three; Cocky Locky, four; Henny Penny, five; Hei! that one I'll snap up."

And so he went on till he had eaten them all up.

The·Sleeping·Beauty

ONCE upon a time, in a far country, there lived a king and a queen who had an only child.

They were so happy when their beautiful baby girl was born that they agreed to have a grand banquet after the christening, and to invite all their friends and relations to rejoice with them.

The chief guests invited to the feast were twelve wise women, who were fairies. The King and Queen asked these fairies to be godmothers to their daughter, in the hope that they would be kind to the little princess, and give her good gifts. To entertain them fitly, the King unlocked the store-cupboard where he kept his treasures—his money, his gold cups and plates, and the best kinds of apples and honey—and took from a shelf twelve golden plates, set with precious stones—one for each of the fairy godmothers to eat from.

59b

Now, there were really thirteen wise women who were fairies in the kingdom; but, as there were only twelve golden plates set with precious stones, the Queen sent no invitation to the thirteenth, who was very old, and who had not been seen outside the tower in which she lived for so many years that no one was sure whether she was alive or dead. The twelve wise women came, and when the feast was over began to give their wonderful fairy gifts to the baby princess.

The first godmother said that she should be as beautiful as the sunrise; the second, that she should be as wise as the years that had gone; the third, that she should be as good as gold; the fourth, that she should be as happy as the day is long; the fifth, that she should be as loving as the angels; the sixth, that she should be as merry-hearted as a lark in the sunshine; the seventh, that she should be as free and strong as the rippling waves; the eighth, that she should be as gentle as the breezes of summer; the ninth, that she should be as graceful as a bird on the wing; the tenth, that she should sing as sweetly as a nightingale; and the eleventh, that she should dance as lightly as a flower in the wind.

The eleventh godmother had just made her gift, when there came into the palace the old fairy who had not been seen for so many years. She was very angry indeed because she had not been invited to the christening feast, and she went straight up to the baby princess, and, stretching out her long, bony forefinger, said:

"The maiden, when she is in her fifteenth year, shall

prick her finger with a spindle, and shall fall down dead!"

This terrible doom brought grief and fear to the whole company. The Queen screamed, the baby cried, and the troubled King knew not what to do; while all the guests trembled. Then the twelfth fairy, who had not yet made her gift, stepped forward.

"I cannot take away that fate," said she, "but I can make it less terrible. The Princess will surely prick her finger with a spindle when she is in her fifteenth year, but she will not die, but will fall into a deep sleep for a hundred years, at the end of which time a king's son shall awaken her. And, when she falls asleep, the whole company at the palace shall sleep also."

Thereafter the troubled King did all he could to save his daughter from the evil fortune foretold by the spiteful fairy. He caused proclamations to be written, ordering every spindle in the kingdom to be destroyed, and forbidding all persons to spin with distaff and spindle, or even to keep them in their houses, under pain of death, until the Princess was fifteen years old. He sent heralds to read these proclamations, in a loud voice, at every street corner in every town and village throughout the kingdom; and commanded that a large bonfire should be kindled in the courtyard of the palace, where he himself watched to see that every woman, young or old, brought her spindle and gave it up to be burned.

As the Princess grew up, it was easy to see that she had

" Let me see if I can work it "

received good gifts from her fairy godmothers; and she was so beautiful, and wise, and good, and gracious, and kind, that all who saw her loved her, and declared that she was the most wonderful princess in the whole world. Her teachers thought it a joy to teach her, her servants ran gladly to wait on her, and her courtiers tried every day to think of fresh things to say or do, to give her pleasure. The people in the streets crowded to see her as she passed, and went away the happier for a sight of her. And her parents said she was a treasure far greater than their whole kingdom and all their riches.

One day, when the Princess was nearly fifteen years

old, the King and Queen went out, leaving her alone. To amuse herself while they were away, she wandered through all the rooms and passages of the great palace, in some parts of which she had never yet been.

In her wanderings she came to an old tower, in which there was a winding staircase, and at the top of the stairs a narrow door. The Princess opened this door and entered a little room, where there was seated a very old woman, busily spinning with distaff and spindle. Now, either this old woman had not heard the King's order for the burning of all spindles, or she was the wicked fairy, who had disguised herself as an old spinner so that she might be sure the Princess would receive her evil gift.

The Princess was surprised to see her and her spinning-wheel. "Well, Granny," she said, "what are you doing here, and what is this strange thing that goes round so fast? Let me see if I can work it," and she took the spindle in her hand. But scarcely had she touched it when she pricked her finger with it; and the next moment she sank upon the floor in a deep sleep.

Then the old woman cried for help, and people came running in alarm to find out what had befallen their Princess. They rubbed her hands, they shouted in her ears, they bathed her forehead with Hungary water, and did all they could think of to rouse her, but in vain; the Princess slept peacefully through all the disturbance.

Then the people knew that she had fallen into the sleep which the twelfth fairy had foretold, and that she would not

The King and the Queen slept upon the throne

waken again for a hundred years. So they carried her to her own room, and laid her upon the bed; and as soon as this was done the King and Queen, the whole Court, and everybody in and about the palace suddenly fell into a deep sleep too.

The King and the Queen slept upon the throne, and the ladies and gentlemen of the Court, some sitting and some standing, slept around them. The guards slept at their posts; the servants fell asleep, quite suddenly, over their work; the cook, who was just about to box the scullion's ears, went to sleep with one arm raised; and the scullion slept with his mouth open, ready to scream. The grooms slept in the courtyard; the horses slept in the stables; the dogs slept in the kennels, or in the palace with their masters; the pigeons slept upon the roof, with their heads tucked under their wings; the flies slept upon the walls; the King's parrot slept upon the back of the throne; and the Queen's cat slept upon the floor. Even the fire upon the hearth left off flaming and crackling and became still, and the spits ceased from turning, while the roasting meats left off hissing and fizzling. Everybody and everything about the palace slept.

And now, all around it, a hedge began to grow. Prickly thorn bushes, with brambles twisted and twined among them, formed this hedge, and it grew so tall and so thick that very soon nothing could be seen of the palace from outside but the vane upon the top of the highest tower.

The story of the beautiful princess who slept within the

thorn-guarded palace, until a king's son should come to awaken her, was told throughout the land; and many brave princes tried to force their way through the prickly hedge to find her. But neither man nor beast could break a way through that hedge, for it was a fairy hedge. Its boughs could not be forced apart, and they seized and held fast all who touched them; and those who were caught, after striving and struggling for a long time, fell and died.

When a hundred years had come and gone, however, the son of a king then reigning came through the land. He saw the tall vane above the high hedge, and asked an old man to what castle it belonged, and how he might reach it. Then the old man, who had heard the story from his grandfather, told him of the beautiful princess who lay sleeping in the palace within the thorn hedge until a king's son should awaken her. " But," said he, " you cannot reach her. Many kings' sons have tried, and all have died in the hedge of thorns."

But the Prince was not afraid. He went boldly up to the immense hedge with his sword drawn, and, because it was now time for the wicked fairy's spell to be broken, the thorns and brambles turned to tall, beautiful flowers as he drew near, and the flowers parted to let him pass through, closing behind him, as a hedge of thorns once more, to keep others from following.

Wondering greatly, the Prince passed on until he reached the courtyard of the palace. Here the grooms lay sleeping; and upon the roof of the palace the pigeons slept, with their heads tucked under their wings.

The Prince gazed a-round him in awe and astonishment; then, fearing to make a sound in the great stillness and silence, he crept onward on tiptoe, past the stables and kennels where the horses and dogs were sleeping, and into the palace, where, in the en-trance, stood the sleeping guards.

Inside the great hall of the palace there was no sound but that made by his footsteps. The King and Queen, the courtiers and servants, still slept.

Quickly the Prince passed them all and mounted the stairs, his heart full of one

He crept onward on tiptoe

great desire—to find the beautiful princess. At length he entered the room where she lay sleeping; and, when he saw her, he stood for a while as still and silent as the sleepers themselves, for she was so beautiful that he could do nothing but gaze at her.

At last he stooped and kissed her; and then the spell of the wicked fairy was broken.

The Princess awoke, and, smiling upon the Prince, said: "Is it you, my prince? I have waited long for you."

And the Prince, delighted even more by her kindness and graciousness than by her beauty, told her that he loved her better than anyone in the world.

Then the Princess arose, the Prince took her by the hand, and they went together down the staircase and into the great hall.

And now the whole company awoke, and looked with wonder around them. The King sprang to his feet with a cry of welcome; the Queen laughed for joy; the courtiers tried to remember what they were just going to do; and the servants hurriedly began to work, each one thinking he had been caught napping. The cook boxed the scullion's ears, and the scullion screamed, and dropped a bowl of soup; the fire began to flame and crackle; the spits began to turn, and the roasting meats to hiss and fizzle. The dogs barked; the cat stretched herself; the parrot screamed; and the flies crawled along the walls. The guards stood to attention, blinking solemnly; the horses neighed, and the grooms ran to feed them; and the pigeons flew down from the roof and pecked up some corn.

Everywhere were life, and stir, and bustle. At the same moment, the whole thorn hedge changed again into beautiful flowers; so the news quickly spread through the land that the beautiful princess had at last been awakened.

The Princess awoke

Then there was great rejoicing in the palace.

All had been silent for so long that everybody had a vast deal to say to everybody else. In the midst of the talking, and laughing, and handshaking, the chief lady-in-waiting announced that supper was ready, and the Prince led the Princess into the great hall of looking-glasses, followed by the King and Queen and the rest of the company, who by this time were all dreadfully hungry.

The supper, which was a very rich feast, was served by the officers of the Court, while the Court musicians played the good old tunes of a hundred years ago.

The Prince and Princess of course sat together, and, as

they ate the splendid dishes that were placed before them, the Princess told the Prince what had happened just before she fell asleep.

Then he told her all that had taken place since; and as some of the courtiers who were near them heard what he said, and passed on the news to their neighbours, soon everyone was talking about, and wondering at, the great changes that had taken place in the world.

After supper the Prince and Princess were married in the royal chapel, by the Lord Almoner; and they lived happily ever after.

ONCE on a time a rich gentleman, unhappy from the death of his wife, resolved to marry again, that his little daughter, whom he dearly loved, might have some motherly care. Unfortunately his choice fell upon a proud, haughty, and selfish woman with two daughters much like herself. Not until the marriage was over did the stepmother show her true temper, and that she could not bear the pretty little girl, whose goodness of heart contrasted with the selfishness and pride of her own daughters. She ordered the child to live in the kitchen, made her work with the servants, and forced her to sleep up in a garret without anything to make her comfortable. When the child had done her work she used to sit in the chimney corner among the cinders; so that she went by the name of Cinderella. And Cinderella, dirty and ragged as she was, was a thousand times prettier than her sisters, drest out in all their finery.

It happened that the king's son gave a ball, to which he

invited all the persons of fashion in the country: Cinderella's stepsisters were of the number. He did not invite Cinderella, for he had never heard of her.

Nothing could exceed the joy of the two sisters; every moment was spent in fancying gowns, shoes, and head-dresses which would set them off to the greatest advantage. They talked of nothing but what they should wear.

On the morning of the ball, while Cinderella was busily engaged in dressing her sisters, they said to her:

"Should you not like to go to the ball?"

"Ah!" said she, "you are only laughing; it is not for such as I am to think of going to balls."

"You are right," said they; "folks might laugh, indeed, to see a Cinderella dancing in a ball-room."

At length the great moment arrived: the proud girls stepped into a beautiful carriage, and, followed by servants in rich liveries, drove to the palace. When they were out of sight, Cinderella sat down in a corner and began to cry.

Her fairy godmother suddenly appeared and asked what ailed her.

"I wish—I w-i-s-h—" sobbed poor Cinderella, without being able to say another word.

"You wish to go to the ball?"

"Alas, yes!" replied the poor child, sobbing still more.

"Well, well, be a good girl," said the godmother, "and you shall go. Run into the garden and bring me a pumpkin."

Cinderella brought the finest one she could. Her god-

" She told Cinderella to lift up the door of the trap very gently "

mother scooped out the inside, leaving nothing but the rind; she then struck it with her wand, and the pumpkin instantly became a fine gilded coach. She next looked into the mouse-trap, where she found six lively mice. She told Cinderella to lift up the door of the trap very gently; and, as the mice passed out, she touched them one by one with her wand, and each immediately became a beautiful horse, of a fine dapple-grey mouse colour.

"Here, my child," said the godmother, "is a coach, and horses too; but what shall we do for a postilion?"

"I will run," replied Cinderella, "and see if there be not a rat in the rat-trap; if I find one, he will do very well for a postilion."

"Well thought of, my child!" said the godmother.

Cinderella brought the rat-trap, which contained three of the largest rats ever seen. The fairy chose the one which had the longest beard; and, touching him with her wand, instantly turned him into a smart, handsome postilion.

"Go again into the garden," she said, "and you will find six lizards behind the watering-pot; bring them hither."

This was no sooner done, than, with a stroke, they were changed into footmen, who all jumped up behind the coach in their laced liveries, and stood side by side as if they had been used to nothing else all their lives.

"Well, my dear," the fairy then said, "is not this such an equipage as you could wish for to take you to the ball? Are you not delighted with it?"

"Y-e-s," replied Cinderella with hesitation; "but must I go in these rags?"

Her godmother touched her with the wand, and her rags instantly became the most magnificent apparel, ornamented with the most costly jewels in the world. To these she added a beautiful pair of glass slippers, and bade her set out for the palace. The fairy, however, before taking leave of Cinderella, charged her on no account whatever to stay at the ball after the clock had struck twelve; as, should she stay but a single moment after that time, her coach would again become a pumpkin, her horses mice, her footmen lizards, and her fine clothes be changed to filthy rags. Cinderella did not fail to promise all her godmother wished, and, almost wild with joy, drove away to the palace.

As soon as she arrived, the king's son, who had been informed that a great unknown princess was come to the ball, presented himself at the door of her carriage, helped her out, and conducted her to the ball-room.

Cinderella no sooner appeared than everyone was silent. The dancing and music stopped, and everybody gazed at the beauty of the stranger. The King himself continually repeated to the Queen that it was a long time since he had seen so lovely a creature.

The king's son conducted her to the most honourable seat, and soon after took her out to dance with him. She danced so gracefully that everyone admired her still more than before, and she was thought the most beautiful and accomplished lady ever beheld. After some time a delicious supper was served; but the young Prince was so busily employed in looking at her that he did not eat a morsel.

Cinderella seated herself near her sisters, paid them a thousand attentions, and offered them a part of the delicacies with which the Prince presented her; while they were quite astonished at these civilities from a strange lady.

As they were conversing, Cinderella heard the clock strike eleven and three-quarters: she rose from her seat, curtsied to the company, and hastened away as fast as she could.

As soon as she got home she flew to her godmother, and, thanking her, told her she would give the world to be able to go again to the ball the next day, for the king's son had entreated her to be there. While she was telling her godmother everything that had happened at the ball, her two sisters knocked a loud rat-tat-tat at the door, which Cinderella opened.

"How late you have stayed!" said she, yawning, rubbing her eyes, and stretching herself as if just awaked out of her sleep.

"If you had been at the ball," said one of the sisters, "let me tell you, you would not have been sleepy; there came thither the handsomest, yes, the very handsomest princess ever beheld! She paid us many attentions, and made us partake of the sweetmeats the Prince gave her."

Cinderella asked her sisters the name of this princess. They replied, that nobody had been able to discover who she was; that the king's son was extremely grieved on that account, and had offered a large reward to any person who could find out whence she came.

"How very beautiful she must be!" said Cinderella. "How fortunate you are! Ah, could I but. see her for a single moment! Dear sister, lend me only the yellow gown you wear every day, and let me go to see her."

"Oh, yes, I warrant you; lend my clothes to a Cinderella! No, no; mind your business, and leave dress and balls to your betters."

The next day the two sisters again appeared at the ball,

and so did Cinderella, but dressed more magnificently than before. The Prince was continually by her side, and said the most obliging things to her, so that the charming young creature was far from being tired; on the contrary, she was so delighted that she forgot the charge her godmother had given her. Cinderella at last heard the striking of a clock, and counted one, two, three, on till she came to twelve, though she had thought that it could be but eleven at most. She got up and flew as nimbly as a deer out of the ball-room. The Prince tried to overtake her; but poor Cinderella's fright made her run the faster. However, in her hurry, she dropped one of her glass slippers, which the Prince stooped down and picked up.

Cinderella got home tired and out of breath, in her dirty old clothes, without either coach or footmen, and having nothing left of her magnificence but the fellow of the glass slipper which she had dropped.

Meanwhile the Prince enquired of all his guards at the palace gates if they had seen a magnificent princess pass out, and which way she went? The guards replied that no princess had passed the gates; that they had not seen a creature but a little ragged girl.

When the sisters returned, Cinderella asked if they had been as much amused as the night before, and if the beautiful princess had been there? They told her that she had; but as soon as the clock struck twelve she hurried away from the ball-room, and, in the haste she made, had dropped one of her glass slippers, which was the prettiest shape that

" Messengers took the slipper"

could be; that the king's son had picked it up, and had done nothing but look at it all the rest of the evening; and that everybody believed he was violently in love with the handsome lady to whom it belonged.

A few days after, the Prince had it proclaimed, by sound of trumpet, that he would marry the lady whose foot should exactly fit the slipper he had found.

Accordingly messengers took the slipper, and carried it first to all the princesses; then to the duchesses—in short, to all the ladies of the Court—but without success. They then brought it to the two sisters, who each tried all she could to squeeze her foot into the slipper; but this was quite impossible.

Cinderella, who was looking at them all the while, and knew her slipper, could not help smiling, and said:

" Pray, let me try it on."

Her sisters burst out laughing. " Very likely," said one of them, "that a clumsy foot·like yours should. fit the slipper of a beautiful princess."

The gentleman, however, who brought the slipper, said that it was but just that Cinderella should have her turn. Saying this, he made her sit down; and, putting the slipper to her foot, it instantly slipped on, and he saw that it fitted her like wax.

The two sisters were amazed to see that the slipper fitted Cinderella; but how much greater was their astonishment when she drew out of her pocket the other slipper, and put it on!

Just at this moment the fairy entered the room, and, touching Cinderella's clothes with her wand, made her even more magnificently dressed than when at the ball.

The sisters immediately perceived that she was the beautiful princess, and at once asked her forgiveness for the ill-treatment she had received from them. Cinderella tenderly embraced them, and said that she forgave them with all her heart.

Cinderella was then conducted to the young Prince, who, finding her more beautiful than ever, instantly desired her to accept his hand.

The marriage ceremony took place in a few days; and Cinderella, who was as amiable as she was handsome, gave her sisters magnificent apartments in the palace, and a short time after married them to two great lords of the Court.